SOLOS
FOR THE
ENGLISH HORN PLAYER

with Piano Accompaniment.

Transcribed and Edited by
THOMAS STACY

G. SCHIRMER, Inc.

DISTRIBUTED BY

HAL•LEONARD®
CORPORATION
7777 W. BLUEMOUND RD. P.O. BOX 13819 MILWAUKEE, WI 53213

CONTENTS

FOREWORD

These arrangements are intended to increase the limited repertory available to the English Horn player. They are appropriate for performance and study at all levels, and cover a wide span, both in technical difficulty and in chronology—Henry Purcell to Erik Satie.

Also included are English Horn solos from the orchestral repertory, which are not beyond the capability of beginning players. Three Baroque sonata transcriptions employ ornamentation of the period.

I have tried in so far as possible to adhere to the original keys and composers' markings.

I wish to express my thanks to Philip Brunelle for his invaluable knowledge and help with the piano reductions.

T.S.

Solos for the English Horn Player

Transcribed and Edited by Thomas Stacy

When I Am Laid in Earth
from: Dido and Aeneas

Purcell, one of England's great composers, concludes his only opera with this passacaglia — a series of variations based on a recurring five measure descending ground bass figure.

Henry Purcell
(1659-1695)

4

Sonata

This sonata was originally written for recorder.

Georg Philipp Telemann
(1681-1767)

Sonata

This work is transcribed from Sonata No. 3 for cello and basso continuo.

1

Benedetto Marcello
(1686-1739)

47409

2

Allegro

3

Grave

p molto sostenuto

p molto sostenuto

col pedale

simile

13

47409

4

Where'er You Walk

from: Semele

Jupiter sings this tenor aria in Act II of the oratorio, *Semele*, composed in 1743.

George Frideric Handel
(1685-1759)

18

Largo

47409

Adagio
K. 580A

Alfred Einstein in his revision of Köchel's catalog of Mozart's works designates this piece (K. V. Anh. 2, No. 94) as originally composed for English Horn and String Trio, rather than Viola, to complete the quartet. The opening section is very similar to the "Ave Verum" which Mozart set for Chorus and String Orchestra two years later in 1789. This *Adagio* is often considered to be a study for the "Ave Verum."

Wolfgang Amadeus Mozart
(1756-1791)

22

B

47409

24

47409

Tristan and Isolde
(Prelude to Act Three)

Richard Wagner
(1813-1883)

Lento moderato

The curtain rises on a delapidated, overgrown garden on a rocky cliff; a wide expanse of sea. Tristan, asleep on a couch under a huge tree, is almost lifeless. Kurvenal, grief-stricken, listens to his breathing. The sound of a shepherd's pipe is heard:

Notturno

This is the third movement of the String Quartet No. 2 in D major. It is also frequently performed by string orchestra.

Alexander Borodin
(1833—1887)

The Swan
from: The Carnival of Animals

In this popular section of "The Carnival of Animals," written in Paris in 1922, the solo line is originally played by cello.*

Camille Saint-Saëns
(1835-1921)

Adagio e tranquillo

★ This work may also be performed by English Horn and Harp.

Largo
from: Symphony No. 9

This work is taken from the second movement of the Symphony No. 9 in e minor, Op. 95, subtitled "From The New World."

Antonin Dvorák
(1841-1904)

B poco più mosso

C Meno Mosso-Tempo I

Sicilienne

The Sicilienne is a 17th and 18th century dance of Sicilian origin. This one was written as an incidental piece to Maeterlinck's play *Pelleas and Melisande*. It is included in the frequently performed "Pelleas and Melisande Suite" with the solo line being payed on the flute.

Gabriel Fauré
(1845-1924)

Allegretto molto moderato

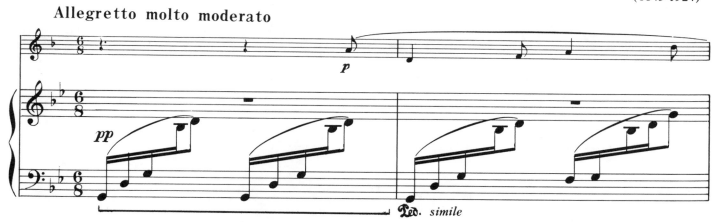

41

47409

The Swan of Tuonela

Sibelius wrote these words in his score:
"Tuonela, the Kingdom of Death, the Hades of Finnish mythology, is surrounded by a broad river of black water and swift currents. On it, in majestic course, floats and sings the Swan of Tuonela."

Jan Sibelius
(1865-1957)

Andante molto sostenuto

D

poco a poco
meno moderato

* Connect all tremolandos.

Gymnopedie No. 2

Gymnopedies, written in 1888, were originally a suite of three pieces for piano. The decoration on a Greek vase, depicting youths performing ancient dances, inspired this slow and measured work.

Erik Satie
(1866-1925)

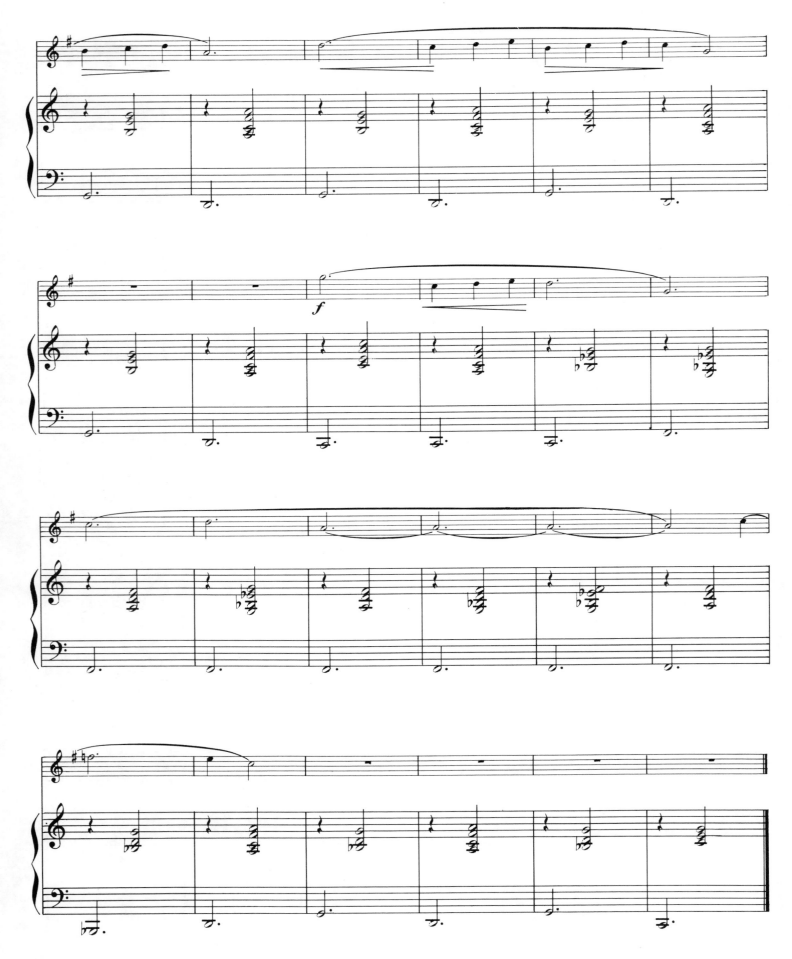

Intermezzo

This well-known orchestral piece was especially composed for the first performance of the opera, *Goyescas,* at the Metropolitan Opera House, New York, January 28, 1916; it is not included in the original score. The characters and scenes of *Goyescas* are taken from the paintings of the great Spanish painter, Goya.

Enrique Granados
(1867-1916)

47409

E

G **Tempo I**

*Finger low E♭, with 2nd Octave key.